RISE TO POWER

CONNOR WHITELEY

No part of this book may be reproduced in any form or by any electronic or mechanical means. Including information storage, and retrieval systems, without written permission from the author except for the use of brief quotations in a book review.

This book is NOT legal, professional, medical, financial or any type of official advice.

Any questions about the book, rights licensing, or to contact the author, please email connorwhiteley@connorwhiteley.net

Copyright © 2024 CONNOR WHITELEY

All rights reserved.

DEDICATION

Thank you to all my readers without you I couldn't do what I love.

CHAPTER 1

A hundred thousand years before the Realm was formed, there wasn't a single grand mighty human kingdom, nor was there the Great Wall keeping the Orks out of the human land, and there certainly wasn't the southern region of the world trapping the trolls and other monsters from destroying the human land.

The world was very different back then and humanity was walking blindly into its own extinction, so a single woman wanted to change the fate of humanity and save everyone. The only problem was that she was a Queen of the weakest kingdom.

Queen Augusta Windsoro sat on her poorly made lumpy golden throne that was a disgrace of a throne if there ever was one. The diamonds, rubies and emeralds that had once been embedded into the golden throne, had now fallen out and been robbed away.

Even the throne room itself was nothing more

than a mere shell of what it had been in her grandfather's time. Augusta still loved the cold rough and chipped stone walls of the small throne room that was barely big enough to fit herself, her three best friends that made up her court and anyone else who wanted to witness the business of the day happening.

Augusta had never liked the floor because it was just so chipped, damaged and it seriously didn't look like a throne room at all. She half expected the floor of a worker's home to look this bad but she never dated utter those words aloud.

Augusta truly loved her amazing people because they were always so kind to her, they loved her and they supported her no matter what, so she did the same to them.

Out of the four kingdoms, her one called Octogi had the lowest level of tax, best level of medical care in the human land but it was also the poorest, and Augusta hated seeing how many of her people were starving.

And the other kingdoms refused to help her.

Augusta looked out the large oval window next to her and focused on the wonderful stone spires of the castle, the little wooden huts of her people and the massive brown streaks in the street. She desperately needed to fix the city's sanitation problem but there was no money.

There was never any money.

The smell of poo, wee and gingerbread filled the air coming up from the city below and it left the strange taste of burnt offerings on Augusta's tongue.

"Your highness," a woman said.

Augusta smiled at her oldest best friend, Chief Witch Savannah Ben and Augusta was so glad to have her in her court. Savannah was wise, fun and very serious when she needed to be but she also knew that her best friend never called her by a title unless it was serious.

At least Savannah had dressed for the occasion by wearing her long white robes and walking around with her official stick that would destroy enemies in a single blast of magical energy. It was a shame that Savannah couldn't leave Octogi because the three other kingdoms hated magic but Augusta loved Savannah all the same.

"Douglas and Ianican cannot join us today," Savannah said trying her best to sound regal.

Augusta wasn't impressed. She needed the advice of the military and Douglas was the best General she had ever had the pleasure of working with. He was diplomatic, skilled and kind. No one understood how hard that was to find in a military man.

It was even worse with the Lord Mayor of the Capital not attending today, Augusta needed to know exactly how the people were doing. Ianican was a good man, if not a little out of touch with the people but she needed all the help she could get.

"Ianican is busy dealing with a group of barons that arrived at the city last night requesting an audience with you,"

Augusta just shook her head. She knew exactly what barons they were and why they were here in the first place. They were the same five barons that had verbally attacked her every single chance they could get over the past two months.

They called themselves the *Freedom Front* barons and Augusta wouldn't have minded if those barons had wanted to become independent from Octogi but there were mines on those lands. And those mines were the only things keeping her economy going.

If she lost the mines, she lost everything.

"And Douglas cannot attend because he... he's dead,"

Augusta laughed out of shock. She had only seen Douglas two days ago when she had sent him to the frontline against the ork invasions to deliver a new supply of weapons.

Of course like everything in Octogi the weapons were badly made, cheap and they wouldn't last long. But it was the best she could do and there were already rumours of a full-on rebellion brewing in the military.

Augusta couldn't allow that at all, not only because she didn't want to be killed but because she knew exactly how the military would rule her country.

There would be massive conscriptions, slave camps and full-on invasions of the other kingdoms and in the end Octogi would be wiped out. Along with all the amazing innocent people that she loved.

She just looked at Savannah. "Tell me about the

other kingdoms. I know you sleep with Harvic he must have told you some intelligence,"

Savannah grinned. "You really do know everyone in the kingdom,"

Augusta didn't have the heart to tell her it was how she had managed to rule for ten years without getting assassinated.

"Longmano's king was killed last week and his son, same age as you has taken up the throne and he is receiving political guests at the moment,"

That wasn't exactly the worse idea Savannah could have suggested. It wasn't like their kingdoms exactly got on but Augusta and the former king did get on well personally, because whilst Octogi was in the north, fighting the orks, Longmano was in the far south of the war constantly fighting trolls, monsters and demons.

Augusta had used that relationship once to get reinforcements for the war against the orks but after a slaughter and all the Longmanoians were killed. The king never sent help again.

"What about Lordigo and Jasper?" Augusta asked really wanting something she could work with.

"You are not going to Jasper and that is final,"

Augusta laughed. She didn't exactly want to go to the richest, most powerful and most brutal kingdom either. Jasper was ruled by a horrible king that had hated Augusta ever since she had come to the throne.

The damn king was always throwing all his weight on the other kingdoms to stop sending food, drink and other supplies to Augusta. She was really looking forward to when the King died but his witches and wizards were far too powerful to ever allow that to happen.

"But you might be able to do something with Lordigo, our good and honourable neighbour because they have a massive problem,"

Augusta leant forward. She had always liked the sound of problems because problems were opportunities.

"Lordigo has recently entered a full-scale civil war between King Alfred and his two sons the Dukes of Grace City,"

Augusta slowly nodded because that really was rather interesting because King Alfred was a... challenging man but he always believed in war over friendships. It was only when her father decided to kill Alfred's wife for the sake of it that Alfred had stopped raiding Octogi.

The sons were also fairly good people and Augusta had even kissed one of them at one of her father's parties, so seeing if she could lean a hand in the civil war might earn her a valuable ally.

"Order the coach I want to make a visit to Lordigo immediately," Augusta said.

Savannah laughed. "August, we cannot just go into another kingdom without permission. I'll contact my counterpart in Alfred's court and get a meeting arranged for tomorrow morning. But what do you plan to get out of it?"

Augusta shrugged as she stood up and realised just how awful the damn throne was as her joints ached and pounded.

"An ally but I'm thinking of unification,"

"I think the sound of that your highness, Queen Augusta of Octogi and Lordigo. That does have a nice ring to it,"

As Augusta watched her best friend leave the throne room and three royal guards wearing dirty gold armour stormed in, she just smiled because that really was a great thing to hear and she hadn't even realised that was what she wanted until it had come out of her mouth.

But why stop at one Kingdom when Augusta could be Queen of all four?

CHAPTER 2

Duke of Grace City, Charleston Alfred leant against the wonderfully warm stone window of his grand Spire in the very middle of Grace City. Charleston seriously loved the wonderful aromas of freshly baked breads, cakes and pastries that filled the aromas from all the delightful business below the Spire.

He had always loved Grace City since he was a child and when his idiot father had gifted it to him as a birthday present at aged ten, Charleston was thrilled with it. He finally owned a city and the most beautiful in the entire country.

He just stared out at the wonderful white marble buildings that looked like they rose out of the ground like plants. From above they all looked like white slabs of marble but Charleston knew from below they looked a lot more precious, artful and simply stunning.

The sound of singing, ringing bells and people

chatting away from in the busy market square echoed around the entire city and that made Charleston a lot happier than he ever wanted to admit. He was still surprised that everyone had supported his rebellion against his father and no one had challenged him.

That was what he loved about his people and that was why his foul father would never be King for a full term. He was cruel, evil and very twisted when it came to "weaker" people.

Charleston focused on the immensely tall solid steel walls that encased the city in a ring of protection, and he really hoped when his father unleashed the full might of the military against him that it just might hold.

His foul father had already sent a few hundred troops to break the city but thankfully his troops had managed to hold it off.

Charleston forced himself to sadly look away from the window and he leant against the cold oak wood of his brown desk, and smiled at his brother who was sitting opposite him in a chair forged from ironwood.

His brother, Owen, looked good today in some leather pants and leather armour and Owen might have been about four years younger than him but he was so glad Owen was okay now. And he actually looked happy sitting there, reading a book and laughing out loud for the first time in years.

Charleston loved his brother's laughter, it was so young, innocent and sweet that he just knew that any man that loved his brother would be very, very lucky indeed.

Charleston hated it how his brother had been beaten black and blue by the servants of his father for being gay. It was all because of the so-called Royal Code that prevented it but Charleston didn't care. His brother was wonderful and he was never going to be king so Charleston just didn't understand why it mattered if he was never going to produce an heir.

All Charleston wanted to do was protect his brother like Owen had protected him tons of times on the battlefield against the horrific armies of Jasper.

"Good book?" Charleston asked as he sat down and picked up a new stack of intelligence reports.

"Yeah. It's a romance book between two princes. Father would have murdered me if he caught me reading it,"

Charleston weakly smiled. He hated that thought with a passion.

"I was thinking I was going to ride out on the crop fields and see how the defences are coming along later. Want to join me?" Owen asked.

Charleston bit his lip. If he was as evil as his father he would have kept Owen trapped in the Spire to make sure nothing could ever happen to him again but he forced himself to smile and nod.

"I'm glad you're happy to go out now," Charleston said forcing the words out. "How are your-"

There was a loud knock on the solid wooden

door to the chamber. Charleston wondered for a moment if anything could actually break that door down, it was so solid.

"Come in," Charleston said.

A few moments later, a very tall woman stormed in in golden armour and threw a piece of parchment on the desk.

Charleston smiled as he read it, it was something about Queen Augusta of Octogi coming to visit King Alfred the next morning.

He had always loved spending time with her as a kid and teenager. There was even a great party between the two kingdoms and Charleston had utterly loved spending the evening with her. She was so wise, kind and she was a sensational kisser.

"Do you think she's a threat?" Own asked.

Charleston laughed. "Definitely not. The Augusta I knew was no danger to good people and I doubt her rule has changed that,"

"But my Lord, she is a Queen of a foreign power. Why is she visiting your father if not to give him strength and support his crusade against us?"

"You don't read politics and many intel reports do you?" Owen asked the woman. "Octogi is not a rich, very successful country. They are invaded daily by Orks and no country helps them,"

"Damn our father,"

"And it even worse that Octogi keeps the rest of us safe. If Octogi falls then all the human lands would be invaded by Orks," Owen said.

Charleston had to admit he didn't know a single thing about that. He was just glad that Owen was a far better person at managing the international affairs of the rebellion.

At the end of the day, Charleston just knew that Owen would make such a better King than him. Owen had the knowledge, skill and passion to help make Lordigo a real powerhouse in the world and maybe they could finally stand up to Jasper.

But that damn Royal Code made that impossible.

Charleston just looked at his brother because he had to leave him for a little bit as much as he hated the notion.

"I need you to rule the City for a little while,"

Owen nodded. "Of course. I'll send more troops and people to work on the farm defences in your absence,"

Charleston laughed. He loved how his brother was always thinking about how to protect the City.

"Should I get the horses for you, my Lord? The woman asked. "And what destination do you have in mind?"

Charleston huffed. "I have to go to the capital and see Queen Augusta for myself. I have to know if she's a friend or foe and what her intentions are,"

And as soon as the words left his mouth Charleston got a lot more nervous. Because he just knew that the arrival of the Queen could save his rebellion or damn them all.

CHAPTER 3

The wonderful aromas of juicy crispy fried chicken, sweet peas and succulent pulled pork filled the air as Augusta sat at the head of her wobbly wooden dining table. When the long black table had belonged to her grandfather it had been the finest table of its day with amazing pieces of art, words and depictions carved into the woods by experts.

Augusta had loved running her fingers over the wood as a child but now they were long gone, all the artwork and other wonderful features of the table had been infected by woodworm and eroded by time.

Thankfully the table was now clean of taint but it was certainly a husk of its former self, a mere wooden table that was probably going to crumble the moment it could.

The staff had been great tonight by covering the table with dirty white tablecloths that had some moth-eaten holes in it, but it did manage to somehow improve the whole look of the dining table.

The immense grey stone walls made the dining chamber look sad, depressed and neglected at the best of times. Augusta was just glad that no one ever wanted to visit her kingdom because she was so poor, at least that way no one dared to see the state of her kingdom.

Augusta focused on the delightful plate of food and the kingdom might have been poor, but Octogi did have some of the best chefs in the human lands.

She had always loved fried chicken and peas and bacon. The chefs used only the freshest oil they could fine and they didn't dare let it go to waste because once it was used, Augusta had ordered it to be added to the boiling pots around the castle.

At least if they were ever invaded the foul enemies would have to enjoy the boiling hot taste of fried chicken as the boiling oil burnt them alive.

"I think that will be a wonderful idea your Highness," a man said.

Augusta smiled at the four people that sat in front of her, there were two men to her left and two women to her right. Everyone was enjoying their dinner and they were discussing all matters of state, love and kingdom.

Savannah was wearing her sensational golden robes for the dinner and she was mainly staying quiet, unlike the other woman sitting next to her. A small little woman that was in charge of all diplomatic things in Octogi, Gracey was a good woman if not a little… not scared to give her own opinion at times.

Augusta really did enjoy both women's company and it was good that the Lord Mayor had managed to come here tonight, and the other man was a surprise guest as well. He was Baron Benic, the leader of the Freedom Front Barons.

She definitely didn't like Benic. He was rude, annoying and a massive pain in the ass but at least he seemed to be somewhat tolerable tonight.

"So you agree to stop your demands in exchange for me putting up taxes for the purpose of a sanitation system?" Augusta asked.

Benic played with his food almost like it was a poisonous threat to him.

"We all know Octogi does not have the expertise for such a system," Benic said, stabbing his food.

Augusta smiled because that was very true but that was the thing that she hated about the Barons and Baronesses. They believed that because she was noble blood so she was stupid or something.

She wasn't. Augusta always had a plan.

"I am aware of that. Yet Lordigo has the expertise we require,"

The entire dining chamber fell silent and Savannah shook her head at her like this wasn't the time to talk about her ambitions.

"You, want to, what?" Benic asked. "You actually want to, talk to those barbarians,"

That surprised her actually. If the Freedom Front Barons actually gotten what they wanted, Augusta had always believed they had wanted to join the kingdom of Lordigo and become part of their kingdom. It was stupid to believe a handful of Barons could become a successful kingdom alone.

Savannah clicked her fingers and small sparkles flew through the air.

"Sorry for the party tricks your Highness but the expertise of Lordigo will not be easy to get. King Alfred knows how weak we are, we have no money to give him and the mines are, questionable of late,"

Augusta forced herself not to grin at that dig at Benic.

"The mines are operating at 100% efficacy. I will not be challenged by some, witch scum,"

Savannah just stared at Benic. "And remember what I can do as a witch scum to people I don't like,"

Augusta tapped her fork elegantly on the side of her plate. "As much as I enjoy these games between you all I want to remind you that King Alfred is at war. War breeds opportunity. Opportunity breeds money. And money breeds power,"

"Of course," Benic said. "You want to take advantage of him,"

Augusta folded her arms. "King Alfred is in no position to argue with me. We still have spare soldiers. He will become an ally or I will see what the Dukes have to offer me,"

She was impressed with when everyone nodded with smiles so large she wondered if their faces were going to break in a second. Augusta had at least expected some kind of resistance.

Benic took a large mouthful of the crispy wonderful chicken. "Fine then your Highness. I vow to you that if you give Octogi a working sanitation system then the Freedom Front Barons will disappear and we will only ever serve *you*,"

Savannah looked like she was about to punch Benic for even suggesting he might be a traitor but Augusta smiled at her. Savannah stopped moving.

"There's a lot riding on tomorrow's meeting," Gracey said. "We better get you educated on customs, beliefs and I'll tell you the weak point of dear King Alfred,"

Augusta weakly smiled as she realised just how much was riding on this single visit. Not only did she need a powerful ally to help reinforce her position and military against Ork invasions, she needed the expertise of the country to get rid of her Baron problem and she seriously needed more money for the kingdom.

So much was riding on this trip. It both excited her and utterly terrified her.

CHAPTER 4

As much as Charleston absolutely hated leaving Owen behind so he wasn't protecting his wonderful brother, he forced himself to glide through the perfectly clean and sterile and sweet-smelling streets of Lord City. It had taken hours upon hours for Charleston to secretly get through all the security points but he was happy to be here now.

The people were so happy, jumping up and down and they were singing at the arrival of the Saviour Queen, and Charleston really wanted the people to be right.

It was so great to see all the men and women and children walking about with a spring in their step in their long white silk robes as they went to main street to catch a mere glimpse of the Queen's stagecoach.

Charleston walked closer to the edge of the wide open street, occasionally bumping into the immense white stone buildings, and even though the Queen wouldn't be here for hours, it was still great to see the city excited.

The air was wonderfully warm with hints of candyfloss, caramel and other sweet delights in the air. People must have been baking to celebrate the arrival of the Queen but Charleston still couldn't understand why they were so excited.

He had managed to catch whispers and joyful conversations about how the Queen was going to depose Alfred and free them all. Charleston doubted that was going to happen but at least it made him feel better about her arrival.

Maybe she actually was a force for good.

As much as he had wanted to bring his guards, top spies and soldiers with him to act as bodyguards, the problem was Lord City was crawling with all sorts of crazy guards and the larger their group the more likely they were to get caught.

Something Charleston flat out couldn't afford.

Charleston pulled his white hood over his head tightly as four golden armour guards slowly rode past on their tall black horses that breathed out fire every so often. Charleston couldn't understand why his father hated magic so much but loved using it every chance he got, even against his own sons.

"Where is Lord Charleston?" a guard shouted.

Charleston forced himself not to stop and everyone else did the same. He didn't know how his father knew he was in the city but they would kill him on-site if he was caught.

Charleston had no idea what friends the rebellion

still had in Lord City. He used to be great friends with a number of military generals, captains and palace guards. They were all probably dead now.

He also got on great with a top-secret gay club on Main Street but he knew that his father had slaughtered everyone inside soon after Owen escaped.

The only other possible option was the prostitute house over on Marple Street but that place would be crawling with corrupt military generals and from what he had heard Madam Rogue was not so popular anymore with any of the military men so she was probably dead and replaced with another prostitute.

"We will start killing people," another rider shouted.

Charleston wanted to come forward but he couldn't get caught under any circumstances. If he was caught then there would be no one left to protect Owen from their father.

No one at all.

Charleston realised there was one other place he could try but there was a chance the woman might kill him on-site or turn him in without a second thought.

Lady Margret of Ashdown was the former Chief Diplomat for his father, a remarkable woman but she had a hell of a temper when it came to anyone associated with Alfred.

The atmosphere turned from happiness to fear as the riders started to jump off their horses and searching people. He didn't have a choice, Lady Margret's house was only a few blocks away up a massive hill at the end of a vineyard. It was the only place he could try and even that might get him killed.

"Traitor," a rider shouted as she slashed the chest of a woman with her sword.

Charleston quickened his pace towards the Vineyard. It wasn't like he had a lot of options and there was no way in hell he could afford to get caught.

So Margret might just kill him instead.

CHAPTER 5

Lord City, the Capital of Lordigo, was so different to the streets of Augusta's own capital city and much of the country for that matter. As the dirty gold stagecoach slowly rode through the capital city, Augusta just stared out of the open windows that had a slight shine to them because the magical shield that Savannah had placed over the coach before they left.

Augusta had so badly wanted Savannah to come but even though King Alfred made a hell of a lot of use out of his own witches and wizards, Savannah's arrival would only make him rageful and the meeting would automatically fail.

Augusta just couldn't believe how stunning the capital city was with its immense white stone buildings, and it was remarkable how the white was actually clean white. There wasn't a single sign or spot or speck of dirt on any of the stone. It was so perfect that the sunlight reflecting off it almost blinded her.

Even the size of the houses, buildings and

businesses was remarkable, Augusta probably could have built ten wooden huts in the space of a single building in Lord City. And there were tens upon tens of healthy people lining the streets waving at her.

Augusta waved at them repeatedly, she smiled and grinned and it was so good to be out again in the human lands.

There was a particular couple that she focused on wearing perfectly clean white robes and the father was holding their boy up above the crowd. He was waving at her like he was her massive fan.

Augusta blew him a kiss and the crowd went wild.

She didn't exactly know why the crowd were so happy to see her but she had spoken to her spies in the city last night. Apparently there was a buzz about the city because some people believed she was going to call out and replace King Alfred.

Augusta had no idea why these people wanted Alfred gone, but again it was another opportunity.

Before her father had died, Augusta had tried to learn everything from him about how to be a good ruler, and there were a few key lessons he taught her. Like it wasn't always about power when it came to being ruler, it was mainly about making sure the people loved and trusted you. Augusta liked to think she had done that perfectly.

Then the next lesson was all about perception. And if these people believed she was a saviour of some sort then maybe this could be a successful trip after all.

"Wow," Gracey said wearing her finest black silk robes she owned (they were black because it showed the dirt less). "Those spies were kidding,"

Augusta nodded slowly. "King Alfred's position is even more dangerous than I thought. He is a king about to lose but I have a job for you please,"

Gracey leant closer. "You don't want me in the throne room with you,"

"No my friend," Augusta said grinning. "I need you to find out the location of the rebels for me please and see if we can get passage to Grace City,"

Gracey frowned and Augusta understood why. Lord City wasn't very far from the border with Octogi and yet they had had to travel through twenty different security checkpoints.

Grace City was half a country away and Augusta had no idea how many check points they would have to past through to get close to it.

"I will do one better for you," Gracey said. "I'm good friends with the old Foreign Minster here in Lordigo. She owns a small vineyard about ten minutes' ride from here, so can I borrow the coach please?"

Augusta laughed. "Of course. But I can only give you a single guard to protect you, we couldn't afford too many and I need them as a show of strength,"

Augusta shook her head as Gracey looked like she was about to burst out in laughter. Augusta knew that the ten guards she had bought with her with their dented dirty armour was no show of strength at all but it was all Octogi had.

She forced herself not to get angry at herself for being the Queen of a poor, weak kingdom that was often the butt of jokes from the other kingdoms.

Augusta just wanted, needed to protect her people and do good by them. She didn't want them to suffer so this trip simply had to go right.

As Augusta returned to waving and smiling at the wonderful people of Lord City that believed her to be some kind of saviour, she felt her stomach twist into agony.

If Alfred saw her as a threat then he would kill her and it wasn't exactly like her kingdom could do much in the way of revenge.

Augusta was the most vulnerable she had ever been and she really wanted this meeting to be over.

CHAPTER 6

Charleston was more than surprised that it had taken him another two hours to get to Lady Margret's house on top of the hill. There had been so many guard patrols that it was impossible to take the routes he normally did to get up to the hills.

He was more than grateful that he managed to get a glimpse of the beautiful, sexy Queen Augusta as her stagecoach (even if it was even fair to call the rotten thing that) pulled into the Palace. Charleston just wanted her to be okay.

He stood outside a very small white wooden door under a wonderfully made thatch roof that created a type of porch area. There were two floating orbs of golden light that bobbed around the porch area and it really made the evening air of the vineyard seem simply magical.

The large rolling hills were filled with stunningly tall and strong grape trees that had a rainbow of different coloured grapes on and Charleston had been so tempted to take some of the grapes to eat but he didn't dare.

Lady Margret was a powerful witch so she had probably set up some kind of powerful alarm system and she probably knew he was here now. Maybe the fact that he was still alive was a good sign or maybe she only wanted him to believe that.

The air was wonderfully warm despite the setting sun and Charleston knocked on the icy cold white door.

Fear gripped him as he imagined Lady Margret storming out and killing him instantly but there was no sign of her yet. Charleston didn't really want to be out here too much longer in case a worker or someone else saw him.

He just couldn't afford to be killed or captured or tortured.

"I hardly expected you to turn up here," a female's voice said into his mind.

"Please let me in. You know I haven't hurt you. I want to help you,"

A strange laughter echoed inside his mind. "That is exactly what your father said to me and now I cannot use physical magic and even this psychic one is torturous,"

Charleston nodded as he realised his father must have cladded her wrists in Magicum, a strange silvery black metal that made using magic an act of torture for its users.

"I'm sorry. I will find a way to help you. I

promise,"

He hadn't meant for the words to be filled with so much emotion, pain and sadness but he had seen exactly what his father did to people he hated. He knew his father did nothing good to people like Margret.

Charleston blinked. He found himself in a different room.

He was surprised to be standing in Margret's kitchen area with fine white marble counters, tables and a large icebox was tucked into one corner of the kitchen. It smelt wonderful of juicy roasted grapes, juicy sausages and creamy mash potatoes. It was delightful.

Then Charleston noticed Lady Margaret herself wearing a blood red robe was standing next to a boiling saucepan that was large enough to feed three people.

"Are you going for three?" Charleston asked.

Margret laughed. "Of course. Your father might have locked me in these bracelets but my power is too great to block out the visions. Someone else is coming to see us tonight,"

Charleston had no idea who else it could be. It clearly wasn't a foe, or maybe it was, and it couldn't be anyone he knew because Charleston hadn't told anyone he was coming here.

"Are you going to kill me?" Charleston asked as Margret started dishing up the sausages, grapes and mash.

"Three or four sausages,"

Charleston had a good look at the sausages that were about the size of his middle finger so they weren't massive, well too massive.

"Four please," Charleston said.

Margret nodded as she dished up three plates. "No. I will not kill you, I gave up on that fantasy a long time ago because you're right. My problem isn't with you or cute little Owen, it's your father,"

Charleston bit his lip. He really hoped that Owen was okay back in Grace City, but he forced himself to focus on the here and now. That was the best way to protect Owen.

"Is Augusta joining us?" Charleston asked.

"Negative but it is good that you still remember her. You two could be a powerful team together, a King of Lordigo and a Queen of Octogi,"

Charleston shook his head. He didn't want to play politics and get with a woman just because of her station and kingdom (not that there was much of a kingdom to have). But she was right though, Augusta was a hot, sexy and very fine woman, seeing her in the Stagecoach had taught him that.

"Why don't you leave this place?"

Margret stared at him. "I cannot. Another gift of your father is a wonderful curse on me so I cannot leave this place. If I do the curse kills you, Owen and my own children,"

Charleston gasped he had no idea that Margret had been trying to protect them both over the years.

And he really wanted Ruby and Jessica to be okay as well, Margret was such a great mother to them that it would be heart-breaking to see them get hurt now.

"And before you ask my children are safe. They might be both be 25 but I still protect them,"

Charleston nodded. He was 28 as was Augusta but it was nice to know that a parent's love should never ever fade.

Someone pounded on the door.

"I wasn't followed I swear," Charleston said.

Margret laughed. "Relax now Charles. That is our guest, the third person to our dinner and the woman that will represent the Queen in our meeting,"

Charleston had no idea what she meant but this excited him a lot more than he ever wanted to admit.

CHAPTER 7

The past two hours had been simply ridiculous and Augusta seriously wasn't impressed with the sheer stupidity of so-called almighty Lordigo. She hardly had a problem with being forced to have a piping hot bath with rose petals, spices and salts (the first hot bath she had had in months) but the hours of forced pray to gods and goddesses that did not exist was beyond foul.

Augusta stood in the very centre of a bright white marble chamber that reflected the flickering candle light so well that she felt blinded. It was pitch black outside but it might as well of been midday or sunrise. It was so damn bright.

A roaring, crackling fire was tucked away behind the imposing and rather scary Black Throne that sat proudly at the head of the throne room. And sitting on there was an old man cladded in full black battle armour carrying two longswords like Augusta was going to kill him.

King Alfred was not a good man and she could see that now in his cold eyes, evil grin and the sheer tension of the room.

This meeting was going to end in something to do with her murder that was a guarantee, and Augusta just wished she had more forces now to not protect herself, but to protect her people from his predations.

"You do not bring me a gift. You do not wear clean clothes to meet me. You do not bring anything but yourself. Pathetic," King Alfred said.

Augusta grinned. Of course she had worn clean white robes and white armour to the visit but he knew that the water of Octogi wasn't as clean as his water. The King knew that was a weakness of the country.

The water of Octogi was perfectly safe to drink or bathe in but it wasn't crystal clean. The river was far too corrupted with the blood of orks, pollution from ork industry and witch cults to be crystal clear. Augusta ordered her witches and wizards to make the water safe enough to drink but even they were not powerful enough to make it crystal clear.

And the damn King Alfred knew that. He knew everything.

"Tell me so-called mighty King, why meet with me then?" Augusta asked.

Augusta asked that to the crowd of servants and so-called plebs that filled the back of the throne room, because she wanted to make a point to them, more than to Alfred himself.

He stood. "Because I want to see the look on your face when I tell you your kingdom now belongs to me,"

Augusta didn't react. There was no reason too. Her people knew she would never ever sell them out so this was just another pathetic plot of a desperate man.

"I doubt that highly," Augusta said. "I am Queen of Octogi and one day I will be Queen of your country. But by my father's blood, it is will not by marrying you,"

Alfred laughed and four golden armoured guards stepped out from behind the throne.

"That is a shame my dear because I will be owning your weak, pathetic and foul kingdom one way or another. Jasper is growing stronger each day and they will conquer the Four Kingdoms if we do not stand together,"

Augusta shook her head. She could see the fear, hatred and terror in Alfred and that only made him even more of a weakling in her eyes.

"And I have already dispatched my army to invade your kingdom. If it refuses my rule then it will burn,"

Augusta just grinned. He was beyond stupid. "And I will enjoy seeing your palace run red with blood as the orks invade and conquer the human lands,"

He didn't comment at all.

"We could have been friends you and me. We

could have joined forces and challenged Jasper directly but you lure me here under the threat of war and now, what? You want to kidnap me,"

Alfred clicked his fingers and the guards stormed across the chamber and encircled Augusta.

"You are a fool," she said. "You are a man in civil war with his sons. You are a man that has a kingdom but no power. You are a man that is a defiler of your gods and goddesses and they will strike you down," Augusta said.

She had no idea if the last part would ever convince him this was the wrong decision but he only laughed.

"The gods and goddesses do not exist. I simply use them as tools of control," Alfred said.

Then Augusta realised he never would have said something as outrageous as that in front of the plebs and other servants. He had spoken those words directly into her mind.

He pretended to be a person that hated magic beyond all else but he was one of them. He was a wizard.

And as the guards gripped Augusta by the shoulders she laughed because Alfred had just made a very fatal mistake.

No one trapped her and tried to take her kingdom.

Now Augusta was going to slaughter Alfred. She only had to escape first.

CHAPTER 8

"Damn it,"

As Lady Margaret said that at the dinner table, Charleston just knew that something had gone seriously wrong. They had all been enjoying the wonderful dinner of sausages, roasted grapes and creamy mash potatoes with the wonderful new guest called Gracey when Margret had looked distant.

Charleston had loved talking with Gracey about what a great ruler Augusta was and they were very interested in working with the Dukes to hopefully conquer the country.

Charleston wasn't exactly sure what beautiful Augusta wanted with his country but he was at least willing to listen to her about her case, and he really wanted to see her again. She sounded just as kind, helpful and intelligent now as she had been back when they were both 18 at that magical party.

"What's wrong?" Charleston asked.

"We have a major problem because I can sense

that Alfred has arrested Augusta and the orders have been sent to invade Octogi,"

Charleston just shook his head. That had to be a lie by Margret to manipulate them or something.

He knew that his father was a right dickhead but invading an independent and peaceful nation was beyond mad, especially one as important as Octogi who everyone knew kept the orks at bay.

"This is way more than your rebellion now," Gracey said in a very diplomatic tone. "The Octogi government is happy to help you and your brother but we need aid immediately,"

Charleston really, really wished Owen was here. His head had always been so much straighter than his when it came to diplomatic affairs.

If Owen was here then he would know exactly what to say, do and pledge in terms of support. Charleston had no experience with this and what if Gracey took advantage of him?

"Fine, what do you want?" Charleston asked.

"We need your rebels to help us defend our borders. I can ride to the border to warn them but we need all the men and women you can spare,"

Charleston hated the sound of that. He wanted his men and women to fight and live through a well planed out strike in Lord City. He didn't want to risk their lives in some forgotten country.

Charleston couldn't believe he had just thought of that. He hoped he had gotten away with the nasty thought but Margret just frowned at him.

"I don't have any men and women with me, but Margret explain to me how magic works again?"

Margret frowned. "Magic is only found in certain women and gay men. It is never or extremely rarely found in straight men,"

Charleston grinned. That was exactly what he wanted to hear.

"I know my brother isn't a wizard but can you, create some kind of magic telepathic bridge with him?"

Margret closed her eyes. "Him being gay should be enough for my magic to combine with his. I just hope he's strong enough in his gayness to leant me his power,"

Charleston bit his lip. That certainly wouldn't be a problem.

"Char?" Margret said in his brother's voice. "What do you need?"

Charleston had no idea how the hell Owen was being so calm about this weirdness.

"Send all available forces to the Octogi border immediately. We need to stop our foul father's invasion. The Queen is kidnapped,"

"Confirmed. I'll lead the strike myself,"

Charleston stood up. "No!"

"You cannot protect me forever. My father will kill me horrifically. The only way I can ever be safe is when he dies. If this helps then I have to do it,"

Charleston saw streams of blood pour out of Margret's eyes and nose and ears. He had forgotten how much agony she must be in.

"Fine. I love you. Stay safe,"

Margret cut the line and frowned at Gracey. "I'm sorry. I can't use any more magic. It will kill me,"

Charleston bit his lip as he saw how burnt and blistered her wrists were where the metal bracelets had been burned on by his father.

Gracey got up and went towards the door. "I'll ride to the border and hope I can beat the army,"

A blood curdling scream ripped through the house and Charleston instantly knew that Augusta's stagecoach and guards were dead and the horses were fleeing into the distance.

Charleston hated the look of fear on Gracey's face as they both realised they were under attack.

"Damn your father," Margret said shutting her eyes and the air crackled with immense magic energy.

People smashed down the door.

Charleston heard Margret scream out in utter agony as a portal opened.

"Find your Queen. Free her. Kill Alfred and make Owen king,"

Charleston wanted to protest as litres of blood rushed out of Margret and formed a blood red portal metres away from him. He didn't dare.

This was the only option.

Arrows flew through the air.

Charleston grabbed Gracey and charged into the portal.

CHAPTER 9

The icy cold air wrapped around Augusta as she sat on the even colder iron floor of the barred metal cage that paraded her out of Lord City. The bars were too thick for her to attack and rip through but that didn't worry her.

Gracey was still hopefully free in the City and Savannah was far too disobedient not to be constantly sensing Augusta's soul to see if she was in danger or not.

As the wide dirt road made the cage bump around as the two white horses rode forward with only three golden armoured men protecting their prisoner, Augusta sat in the centre of the cage and focused.

They were currently travelling through a perfectly flat plane of Lordigo that went a lot deeper into the country and away from the border with her own kingdom. All Augusta wanted, needed was for her own people to be okay.

Augusta would have happily died if it meant her people lived freely and how they wanted to, but right now her death would serve no purpose. She had to escape and she needed to save her people.

Augusta focused on her fear for her people and the incoming invasion just in case Savannah was watching her soul. She had no idea how it worked but Savannah often described it as a candle flame that was still and bright when happy, but flickering and dim when she was scared.

Augusta imagined the candle in her mind and make it flicker so fast that it was about to go out.

A sharp bump and jerk of the cage made Augusta lose focus and the guards laughed as she fell forward.

Augusta had to escape but there was no one here to help her and she also knew that the nearest prison wasn't within a three day's fast ride so she was going to die on the way there.

She was going to die no matter what happened.

The air crackled with magical energy and Augusta stood up going over to the front of the cage within an arm reach of the guards.

There were blood red lightning strikes forming and peppering the ground until a fully blown portal appeared.

Augusta wished she had a weapon. She didn't.

Augusta reached forward to grab a guard. She couldn't reach them.

Two people leapt out of the portal. Augusta recognised them. She actually recognised Gracey. And there was a familiar man.

Oh. That was Charleston and wow.

Augusta couldn't actually believe how hot he was. The guards shouted.

The guards stopped. They whipped out their swords.

Augusta took off her shoes. She threw them at the guards. Both shoes struck them.

The guards cursed at her. Two of them went round the back of the cage.

They were shouting at her. Augusta realised she was stupid.

The other guard was attacking Charleston. Augusta couldn't focus on him.

The two men opened the cage. They climbed inside. They raised their swords.

They swung.

Augusta dodged them. Gliding through the air.

She leapt over them. Hitting the barred roof of the cage. The guards laughed at her.

They grabbed her hair.

Pinning her against the front of the cage. They kept laughing at her. Augusta tried to fight.

Their heads flew off them and their corpses landed with a thud and Augusta just grinned as she saw the most beautiful man she had ever seen.

The taste of metallic blood formed on her tongue but she didn't care as she stared into the beautiful deep emerald eyes of Charleston Alfred. When she last knew him he was a skinny twig of a teenager that was barely 18. She was the same.

Yet time had certainly fleshed him out into a real hunk with muscles and a face that was all lines and angles and it was beautiful. Stunning even.

"Lovebirds," Gracey said, and Augusta realised that he was staring at her too and his mouth had actually dropped.

Augusta forced her mouth to work and after a few moments it did.

"Thank you mighty Duke for the rescue," Augusta said. "Me and my country are most grateful but I have get back to them. My people are in danger,"

Augusta pushed pass Charleston and Gracey and climbed out of the cage. She went to the front and unclipped the horses. It had been ages since she had ridden but she remembered the basics.

"I have already summoned my brother and my forces to ride to the border," Charleston said.

Augusta just froze. She had never believed in gods or goddesses but she really looked at the cute innocent man standing in front of her. That single precious night that they had spent together he had told her how his father beat poor Owen constantly. Almost hourly.

"How, how is he? Please tell me he escaped. If not my country will help. He must be freed,"

Augusta hadn't meant to sound so desperate but she had only met Owen once for a minute and even though he moved so awkwardly (probably because of bruises and broken bones) he had been so kind to her and he didn't care that Octogi was poor.

Owen had only ever cared about *her* and *her people*. Just like his older brother.

Charleston hugged her and Augusta loved the immense warmth of the hug and then she felt Charleston freeze, break it and hurry away.

"I'm sorry your majesty. I didn't mean to-"

Augusta waved him silent. "I presume your brother is safe for that kind of reaction but we need to work together. And let's stop with the royalty talk until your father is dead,"

Augusta could tell he was shocked by the suggestion at his father's death.

"Your father attacked my kingdom, he kidnapped me and he tortured your brother. Those are crimes punishable by death in all human lands and I will be the one to enforce them,"

She could tell that Charleston wanted to hug her again but as howls and sounds of battle horns screamed out over the plane. She knew they had to get moving before whatever bandits or enemy forces on the planes found them.

Gracey climbed on a horse. "Here your highness,"

Augusta took her hand and climbed on, wrapping her hands tightly around Gracey.

She was glad that Charleston climbed on another horse as well and as they rode off into the darkness she was looking forward to spending time with the beautiful man from that party.

But she was more than a little concerned about the dark shapes she saw riding about in the darkness.

CHAPTER 10

As Charleston sat on the cold hard ground in the pitch darkness with him only barely being able to see beautiful Augusta and Gracey in the very dim moonlight, he couldn't believe what the hell had happened over the past few hours.

The three of them were sitting at the bottom of a very steep hill that thankfully blocked out the harshness of the icy cold wind that had pounded into them as they rode.

They had been doing that for hours and Charleston had no idea what their destination was, so he only wanted to rest for a few minutes. They needed a plan.

Charleston hated it how there was no way for them to get to Grace City in the pitch darkness and they would have to travel across the entire country to get to the border. But by then Octogi might be saved or dead.

They needed a much better plan and Charleston

didn't have an idea for one at all. He was still so shocked that amazing Lady Margret had actually sacrificed herself for him. She really was amazing.

"We need to kill your father," Augusta said.

Charleston was still so impressed by how calm, beautiful and stunning she looked. He wasn't that calm and his heart was starting to beat faster and faster.

"We also need to know who will replace him," Gracey said.

Charleston nodded. "That is simple. Me or Owen will replace him but I don't want to be king and the people… they love my brother but making him King, that will anger them too much,"

Charleston seriously hated saying the words but it was a very, very unfortunate truth.

Augusta leant forward. "What would your people say if I became their ruler and Owen was, more of an official take-carer but a king in reality,"

Charleston had to admit that would probably work. The people had already showed a strong interest in Augusta (and why wouldn't they she was stunning) so the people might believe Owen was acting on her behalf.

"I can work with that and I cannot see Owen having a problem with that, your highness,"

A loud roar echoed around the plane and Charleston bit his lip. The wolves must have come down the mountains in the far west, they had to get moving before the wolves found them.

Charleston gestured Augusta and Gracey to get back up on their horse and thankfully they did. He did the same.

"We need to ride to a nearby cache of weapons and armour I have. Then we can sneak back into the City and try to assassinate my father,"

"Negative," Augusta said. "I think an uprising might be more effective,"

Charleston shook his head as another massive roar ripped through the plane.

"It makes diplomatic sense and an uprising will draw the focus away from Octogi," Gracey said.

Charleston had no idea if these crazy women were right or wrong. He wasn't a king, a diplomat or anything. He was just a man that wanted to protect his brother and kingdom at all costs.

And if causing an uprising meant that Owen could be safer then Charleston had to do it. At least die trying.

"Fine then. We ride until we reach the cache and-"

A deafening roar ripped through the plane and the wolves howled in utter fear as Charleston realised that was the sound of a dragon.

Charleston had only heard of dragons and they were mainly in Jasper and Longmano. Dragons never ever came this far east before.

He bit his lip as an immense sweeping dragon with two massive wings, a very long tail and a spear-like head blocked out the full moon for a brief moment.

Charleston started to ride off with his horse. The others joined him.

Fireballs rained down at them.

Charleston's horse went mad. It threw him off.

The horse ran away. Augusta's horse did the same.

Fireballs smashed into them. The horses moaned. The dragons chomped on them.

Augusta grabbed him. The three of them ran in the opposite direction.

An immense gush of wind knocked them down from behind.

Charleston turned onto his back and he just froze as the massive dragon stalked towards them.

Charleston focused on its awful black shiny scales, its long dagger-like teeth and the dragon opened its jaws up almost like a smile.

I should have expected Alfred's children to fight better.

The words echoed in his mind and Charleston realised that his father had always loved dragons. What if he had captured one or two or even three?

The dragon flew at them.

Charleston reached for a sword he didn't have.

The dragon screamed in agony.

Charleston watched as a light blue dragon slammed into the black one. The blue dragon smashed its wings into the black dragon's.

The blue one smashed down its jaws on the black one's neck and Charleston had never ever heard of a dragon killing its own before.

Charleston went over to Augusta and held her tight, he loved the feeling of her warmth against him but they all just focused on the blue dragon as it smiled at them.

"What's up mates?" the blue dragon asked. "Sorry about me killing me bruh. He was a nightmare and he was gonna kill ya,"

Charleston was surprised at the creature but he was even more surprised when Augusta stood up, bowed to the creature and placed her arm out in front of her.

Then she simply went over to the creature and touched its nose. The dragon seemed to shiver in pleasure as Augusta stroked the dragon's nose and they laughed together.

"Have you ever encountered a dragon before?" Charleston asked.

Augusta slowly nodded. "Once. I was twenty at the time and I was on a visit to Jasper, some nonsense to do with trade talks and Emperor Jasper showed me his most prize dragon. He normally showed people to his dragon for them to be killed but the dragon refused to kill me. It liked me too much,"

"I can understand why mate. You're a cool girl,"

Charleston really didn't think he would ever get used to the dragon speaking so common but he knew that dragons never revealed themselves free of charge.

The dragon wanted something and dragons always had a dangerous price.

And Charleston really didn't want beautiful Augusta to get hurt.

CHAPTER 11

Augusta was so wonderfully surprised at the beautiful dragon as she brushed her fingers on its perfectly warm snout, and it had been far too long since she had seen such a wonderful creature. She had always loved dragons and it was just a shame that Octogi didn't have any.

But she wasn't as stupid as the dragon believed and she had no idea how but she sort of believed that she could feel what the dragon felt. The dragon felt confident, at peace and happy when she was touching him.

And it was a him.

Augusta had only ever met female dragons before but this male one felt different. Like there was a lie that he was trying to keep hidden from her. She knew that he wanted something, something that he didn't want to know but she was going to have to find out.

She was really impressed with how Gracey

was handling herself, and Charles was just as stunning now as he had been earlier. He was perfect.

"What are you hiding from me?" Augusta asked.

The dragon looked confused.

"Come on," Charleston said. "We all know dragons do not show themselves or help without a fee or something. What do you want?"

The dragon lowered his head as he was level with Augusta. The dragon looked so kind, gentle and wonderful that Augusta was tempted to drop her guard but she didn't dare.

"I want my people to be free and I know what you seek Augusta," the dragon said, his voice becoming firmer and clearly the common talk was a facade.

"So you now reveal yourself," Gracey said.

"My people are mainly kept in cages in Jasper and even Longmano doesn't respect us. I know you, your highness seeking unification of the human lands. Is this truth?"

Augusta really didn't want Charleston to find out like this. He could react badly, he could refuse to help her or he could refuse to help her kingdom against his father but most importantly Augusta just wanted to spend a little more time with him.

Charleston was so beautiful.

"It is true and I want Lordigo to become the first stepping stone in my new kingdom," Augusta said, forcing the words out.

Charleston took a few steps closer to her and Gracey silently followed him as if she could stop him if he attacked her.

"I presume dragon," Augusta said. "If my plan is successful you want my word that the dragons will be free and humans will no longer enslave your kind,"

"Your word,"

Augusta looked away from the dragon for a moment like she was actually having to consider this. Of course she would outlaw it immediately as soon as Jasper somehow became hers but if being Queen had taught her anything it was that it was always good to make it look like you have to carefully consider everything.

"I agree to your terms in exchange for you helping me,"

The dragon grinned.

Augusta looked at Charleston and Gracey and thankfully both of them were smiling. It was brilliant that they now had a dragon ally.

"And my people," Charleston said, "love dragons and the local religion makes it clear that dragons are gods incarnate. Having a dragon with you will help you win people over,"

Augusta nodded that was great news.

She went over to the side of the dragon as if she was going to climb him, something she wasn't sure on yet, but her hand stuck to the dragon.

"What?" the dragon asked.

Augusta tried to pull away but she couldn't. Even the dragon seemed confused by it.

Augusta screamed out in agony as her hand burned and the dragon hissed in pain.

Her hand was released from the dragon and she fell to the ground.

Charleston and Gracey rushed over but Augusta just focused on her hand. There was a very large dagger symbol burnt into her hand and the dragon was shaking its head.

What is this? What has the silly woman done to me?

Augusta was so confused.

What? Why am I detecting her confusion? I cannot be in some human's thoughts or that rubbish. Humans are terrible creatures inside their own heads.

"I, I can hear you I think," Augusta said. "I think we can read each other's thoughts,"

No, no, no. That human cannot be right. I don't want her to read my thoughts, what about if I see a hot dragon?

"If you do see a hot dragon please don't direct those thoughts at me,"

"You, you actually can hear my thoughts. Can't you?" the dragon asked.

"Oh I know what this is," Gracey said. "Savannah spoke about this once, it's been theorised that human can magically bond with the soul of a dragon to create an unbreakable bond. This is the first time it's actually happened,"

Augusta just shook her head. She didn't want to be bonded to a dragon for life, she had read the exact same articles and papers and this, this couldn't be right.

A deafening trumpet horn ripped through the area and the sound of hundreds of horses pounding the ground came towards them.

"Climb aboard," Augusta said climbing on the dragon. Charleston and Gracey joined her.

Augusta leant closer to the dragon's ears. "Please protect us and you have my word your people will be free,"

The dragon reared up its head, unleashed a torrent of fire in utter happiness and Augusta laughed like a little schoolgirl as the dragon flew them away from the invading soldiers.

But Augusta still had no idea at all how they were going to confront and ultimately kill King Alfred.

RISE TO POWER

CHAPTER 12

Charleston clung onto Augusta's fit sexy body for dear life as they zoomed over all of wonderful Lordigo towards the Octogi border.

As the strange dragon zoomed through the air, Charleston seriously wasn't sure what the hell they were meant to do. He certainly didn't like the idea of flying about like some strange bird. This wasn't normal but they had a country to save and an evil king to defeat.

Charleston just wished beyond all hope that Owen was okay and his friends and fellow rebels were okay too.

From high above the pitch darkness of Lordigo appeared so alluring and scary and terrifying almost like all of his friends were dead but the burning fields ahead of them told Charleston everything he needed to know. He heard the screams, shouts and smashing of swords together.

And he just knew that the battle was still raging

on.

Gracey held him even tighter and as much as Charleston wanted to do the same to Augusta, he really didn't want to be seen as clingy. She was so hot and perfect but he didn't want to be needy.

"Cargo take us down,"

Charleston had no idea when she had learnt the dragon's name but the dragon shook his head.

"Negative ma. Enemy forces are too thick and I cannot make a clear attack run on the King's forces,"

Charleston couldn't believe how well connected they already were after only ten minutes of flying but maybe that was something to do with the bond.

"I have another idea. Get us low enough for my forces to see me,"

"Confirmed,"

Charleston held Augusta tight and loved the feeling of her against him as Cargo banked hard right and descended towards the ground.

The air changed and was filled with hints of death, gunpowder and burnt magic. They certainly weren't in Lordigo land anymore. The enemy had forced its way into Octogi.

Charleston hissed as his feet kicked an enemy soldier in the head.

The entire battle stopped and Cargo landed in a clearing with the enemy Lordigo soldiers in their golden armour and golden swords in front of them. And then there were battered, bruised men and women behind them with shovels and pitchforks.

Charleston was amazed the Octogians had lasted this long. He didn't know if they were lucky or just furious foes on the battlefield.

The entire battle stopped and Augusta stepped off and Charleston followed her taking out his sword to protect her at all costs.

Cargo reared his head as high as he could and Charleston really respected him for that. He was clearly on their side now.

"King Alfred is a magic user," Augusta said and Charleston was shocked by the news but he knew she wouldn't lie.

There were little pieces of arguing amongst the enemy but Charleston was glad that some people wanted to listen to her.

"I am Queen Augusta of the Kingdom of Octogi and I do not want this battle to be your last. I want you all to live, serve and protect the people of your kingdom,"

"This won't be our last. We're going to gut your kingdom," someone shouted.

Charleston was impressed how Augusta nodded like the man actually had a valid point and like he wasn't some dumb fool that the military had trained.

"Very true. That is a great idea and thank you for sharing. Just, just don't fight me and my people on some strange orders from a man that hates you all. If you want to fight and die here tonight then please do it, but ask yourself, is this what you really want?"

Charleston was flat out amazed at how Augusta

was talking to them. He had trained in the Lordigo military for years and he had never ever heard of a commander or his father talk to them so respectfully.

Augusta turned towards her military and smiled at them all and they grinned at her. It had to be some kind of secret language because they all laid down their hands and they sat on the floor.

Charleston even felt his own need to put away his weapon and join them but he didn't dare. He still really, really wanted to protect his brother and Augusta first of all.

Augusta looked at the enemy. "You have my permission. If you can attack me and kill me if you can honestly look me in the eye and tell me that the death of my peaceful people is just,"

To Charleston's amazement everyone looked at each other and they looked so unsure that they actually put away their weapons.

"Oh let me through," a man shouted.

Charleston watched as the crowd moved as the man pushed his way towards Augusta but the moment he stepped out away from them.

Someone fired an arrow and killed him. It wasn't an Octogian or a rebel, it was one of the soldiers themselves.

A very short woman wearing golden ornate armour stepped out of the group and smiled at Augusta.

"Your highness, you have a lot of ways with words. Are you going to let my people go or are we prisoners of war?" the woman asked.

Charleston loved it as Augusta did that weird little thing of hers when she pretended to look away as if she was making an impossible choice but she wasn't. Charleston couldn't believe how amazing she was.

"That is your choice my friend," she said. "You can go and be free or return to your King as a failure,"

The woman laughed and walked away. "Come on peeps. I think Longmano is looking for hired guns,"

Charleston took a step forward. "Actually Commander, if the Queen allows it. I would ask if you would join us in marching to Lord City and arresting my father,"

The woman stopped, grinned and looked at her forces. All of the men and women in their golden armour looked at her.

Charleston had no idea who the commander was, she had to be new, but she clearly had the respect of her soldiers.

"What do you say your highness?"

"I would love the company,"

All the former Lordigo men and women cheered and punched the air and Charleston actually had no idea what Queen-magic he had just witnessed. He knew that it wasn't magic but it might as well have been.

And whatever doubt he had about Augusta being able to rule all of the human lands was gone. She truly was amazing and Charleston realised he had missed something extremely deadly.

"Where's my brother?" Charleston asked himself. He hadn't seen him at all. "Where's my brother!"

The Commander frowned. "I'm so sorry Duke. I captured him earlier and ordered him to be taken back to the City for your father's... enjoyment,"

Charleston so badly wanted to kill her but he forced himself not to.

But he had failed. His brother was now captured and now his foul father was going to torture, beat and probably mutilate his precious little brother all over again.

CHAPTER 13

Augusta flat out couldn't believe just how much bigger this plot was than she had first realised. She had wanted to come here to get some expertise, some soldiers and some support for her war against the Orks. She had no idea that she was going to be involved in a civil war, a rescue mission and end up with a wonderful dragon.

"Feeling's mutual," Cargo said.

Augusta laughed. As her, Charleston who was looking really sexy in his silver battle armour and Cargo were zooming over the early morning sky.

Augusta had barely slept but she had zoomed home first, picked up her ornate dirty golden battle armour and she was now flying towards Lord City.

The wind howled past her and whilst even the military that now contained both the Octogi and Lordigo army, were only a few hours behind. When she got to Lord City it would only be the three of them until help arrived.

And Augusta really didn't know if the people were going to be as wise as the army. Granted it wasn't exactly the people that concerned her, it was the Palace guards and all those people closest to King Alfred.

"There," Charleston said. Augusta really loved the warmth of his breath on her ear.

Augusta saw he was pointing towards Lord City that was nothing more than hundreds upon hundreds of tiny little golden lights with some spires rising into the air.

A strange banging sound filled the air. It wasn't drums or warning signs of an attack. Augusta knew that sound all too well.

This was something else.

An immense black iron arrow flew past.

These were damn dragon defences.

Cargo screamed. A black arrow smashed into his chest.

Augusta screamed in pain. Her own chest felt attacked. Charleston hugged her tight.

Cargo flew wildly. Dodging shot after shot.

All the spires were firing at them. Augusta forced herself to focus. She had to help Cargo.

Without knowing how she simply absorbed all the pain and agony that Cargo was feeling. Cargo flapped his wings stronger.

He was recovering but cold fearful sweat poured down Augusta's face. She wasn't used to feeling this much pain.

Charleston held her tight.

Cargo corkscrewed through the air.

Another black arrow slammed into his chest. Slicing into his right wing.

Augusta screamed as crippling pain filled her right arm. The arm felt broken but she knew it wasn't.

Cargo zoomed towards the ground. Barely able to land just outside the City's black stone walls before Cargo collapsed and breathed fire into the gaping hole on his wing.

Augusta climbed off quickly and whipped out her swords as she noticed the City gates were right in front of them.

The immense gates opened and tens of soldiers poured out. All wore golden armour and carrying massive longswords, perfectly crafted crossbows and even something that looked like a gun.

Augusta was so looking forward to having this sort of technology when she was Queen of this land but she had to survive first.

Then Augusta gasped as King Alfred stepped out of the City wearing bejewelled golden ornate armour that glowed bright in the early morning sunlight.

Augusta placed a loving hand on Charleston's wrist. She couldn't have him striking the King for now not when the enemy soldiers were so close to them.

Then she noticed that Alfred's right hand was covered in traces of blood.

"Oh yes Charles. This is most certainly your

brother's blood. I admit he seems stronger than he was when he escaped. But I will break him and it will all be because you are nothing but a failure,"

Augusta was so looking forward to killing him but all the soldiers raised their crossbows at her.

Two or three shots her weak armour could survive but there had to be easily twenty to fifty crossbows raised at her.

"I will release your brother and give him Forever Freedom if you agree to a single condition," Alfred said.

Charleston shook his head. "No condition of yours is ever true,"

Alfred nodded. "I simply require you to get a woman pregnant, make sure she delivers the baby and then you need to renounce your claim to my throne,"

Augusta had to admit that was a foul plan and it just went to show exactly what Alfred was actually after here. All he wanted was an heir to the throne, he didn't want himself to become immortal, he only wanted his Royal House to continue.

"But your highness," Augusta said the phrase feeling weird on her tongue, "if you allow Charleston to take the throne himself then he will continue your Royal House,"

"Liar," Alfred said. "My son has no intention to be King and as for the pussyboy Owen, he will never be a suitable King,"

Augusta just shook her head. "Then you are a fool. Cargo!"

Nothing happened.

Augusta spun around and saw two soldiers standing over Cargo as he was asleep. Yet the soldiers were holding something, a kind of red crystal in front of his nose.

They had knocked him out damn it.

"Arrest them. Take the false Queen to Owen in the dungeons. She's beautiful enough maybe she can cure his illness. Take Charles to his old room. I have a woman for him to impregnate,"

Augusta just couldn't believe what was happening here but if everything that beautiful Charleston had told her was true about Owen. Then she was going to be perfectly fine because together Augusta had a feeling that they would be truly unstoppable.

She was a lot more concerned about Charleston as they both stared into each other's eyes and Augusta just wanted him to be okay.

But the army would be here in a few hours. Augusta just had to make sure she was still alive for then.

As impossible as that was going to be.

CHAPTER 14

As the guards threw Charleston into his old bedchamber that was nothing more than a King size bed without any sheets, pillows or anything else in it. He had to admit that his father was completely mad now and he seriously had to get out of here.

He knew that there would be guards outside and all the hidden weapons he had once kept in here were clearly gone. It was only him, the bare stone walls of the room and the bed.

Charleston just shook his head when he realised there was a female prostitute in his bed. She was about the same age as him, barely wearing very bad clothes and she looked awful. Her teeth were black and everything.

"Hello sweetie-pie," she said as she went over to him and started playing with his white tunic he had been wearing under his armour.

That was yet another thing that he needed to find. He had to find his armour, find beautiful

Augusta and his brother and then kill his father.

The woman pushed him against the wall and started kissing his neck.

Charleston pushed her away and looked at her.

"Please. You don't have to do this," Charleston said.

He was seriously hoping he could appeal to her humanity and get her to stop forcing herself on him.

Charleston wasn't turned on at all by this nightmare.

The woman let out a cackling laughter and her eyes twisted into those of a madwoman. She jumped up.

She charged at him.

Pinning him against the wall and grinding herself against him.

"Stop this. Please. I don't want to hurt you," Charleston said.

The woman punched him and went to grab his balls but he charged forward.

Throwing her off balance. She landed on the ground and she was about to get up but Charleston knocked her out cold.

He seriously hadn't wanted to do that but he had more concerning things now. He had wanted to help the woman as a partner and friend, he could have gifted her anything in the kingdom but she was clearly a madwoman in the end.

Charleston really hoped she never ever woke up. He had given her two chances to stop and she had ignored them both. Anyone, man or woman, who did that deserved to die.

Now Charleston had to deal with the guards.

"Help!" Charleston shouted. "The woman. She's dying,"

Charleston rushed over behind the wooden door to the chamber. The door gently swung open and the two soldiers rushed towards the woman.

Charleston charged at them. Smashing their heads together.

Someone unsheathed their sword behind him.

Charleston ducked. A sword rushed past.

Charleston leapt up. Kicking the last man in the knee.

He collapsed to the ground. Charleston grabbed the sword of another guard and rammed it through his thick head.

Charleston looked at the woman and as much as he wanted her to suffer for going against his wishes. He just knew that she was a madwoman that needed *help* not punishment.

Charleston grabbed another sword so he was wielding two and then he ran off down the massive stone corridor outside his chamber.

The corridor was so dark, dim and awful compared to his teenage years. The castle felt a lot more depressed as Charleston continued down the corridor.

There were a bunch of wooden doors that led to other chambers but Charleston knew that they were all empty. It seemed that everyone had fled this section of the castle.

Charleston hooked a right and smiled when he saw a very dark staircase that would lead him directly to the dungeons. And because it wasn't the main entrance it would be less well-defended.

A massive snarl came from behind him.

Charleston spun around and frowned. There was a massive Dire Wolf snarling at him. It had to be double the size of him and each fang had to be the size of his legs.

The wolf charged. Charleston leapt out the way.

He rolled on the floor.

The wolf smashed into him. Throwing him against the wall.

One sword flew out of his grip.

Charleston charged at it. Swinging his sword. It did no damage.

The Wolf flew at Charleston.

The wolf rammed him against the wall. The coldness burnt him.

Bright white crackling energy formed around the wolf. The wolf got bigger and bigger.

The wolf opened its jaws.

Charleston punched the beast in the eye. The wolf released him.

Charleston ran down the corridor. He doubted the wolf could follow him into the dungeons. They would be too narrow.

Charleston almost made it to the stairs. A strange

force grabbed him.

Throwing him into the jaws of the wolf.

He felt the creature about to chomp down on him.

Charleston swung his sword.

Jabbing the creature in the eye. It did nothing.

Charleston saw the creature's jaw about to rise up.

Charleston slammed his sword into the wolf's fangs.

The fangs shattered like glass. The wolf dropped Charleston.

Charleston ran away as the wolf slumped to the ground. Snarls and hisses of pain filled the corridor.

So Charleston picked up the sword he had lost earlier and as much as Charleston knew it was a risky move he knew that he just couldn't leave the animal in pain.

So he slowly went over to the wolf as it cried and tears filled its ears in agony and Charleston pressed the swords against its eyes.

He pressed them in. Killing the poor wolf that his father had manipulated into becoming a mindless killing machine.

Charleston went down the stairs into the pitch black darkness of the dungeons.

Charleston had to find his brother, Augusta and kill his father. There was nothing more important now.

CHAPTER 15

Augusta was absolutely amazed at how wonderfully intelligent Owen was, despite him being turned black and blue by cuts, bruises and harsh beatings by his father. Owen have had a split lip and cuts but Augusta was seriously impressed as they both tried to work out how to escape the prison cell.

The problem was that the damn prison cell wasn't made from blocks of stone like all the other prisons in the human lands. This prison cell was carved out of solid granite so there was no way in hell that there were any other ways to escape besides from the immense cold iron bars that formed a solid wall in front of them.

Augusta wanted nothing more than to simply smash down the walls with a mere punch but she didn't have any magic, she certainly wasn't that strong and she knew she was simply growing desperate.

The darkness of the dungeons was also annoying her greatly. There were stupid little orbs of glowing light above them in the cell to give them some kind of light but the cold stone corridor outside of the cell was shrouded in pitch darkness.

And it was shrouded. Augusta could see the little tendrils of darkness dance in the air and she was starting to believe that the orb of light might just be the only thing stopping the tendrils from attacking them.

"Here," Owen said.

Augusta looked at what he was looking at and she couldn't believe how for the past few hours as her and Owen had searched every inch of this place, she hadn't noticed the actual metal barred door of the cell had open-top hitches.

In other words if she could only get enough leverage then she could literally pop the doors open.

"You don't happen to have a crowbar in your armour do you?" Owen asked.

Augusta was about to laugh when she realised that she was still in her battle armour because the guards doubted it was anything more than paper thin. Actually it wasn't.

She had to admit that whilst her kingdom didn't have any forge masters or anything mastercrafted because of how poor Octogi actually was. This battle armour had been forged in Jasper and gifted to her grandmother as a gift.

That was back when Jasper had tried to unite the four human kingdoms under Jasper's foul banner. Thankfully they failed but she wasn't going to.

Augusta got on the ground and wedged one arm through the metal bars of the door like she would a crowbar and then she placed her other arm under it, so it acted like a leverage point.

"Of course," Owen said. "That is brilliant. You start leveraging it and I'll catch it,"

Augusta was really glad he was here, she actually hadn't even thought about catching the metal door before it fell on top of her and killed her.

She started to leverage it off the hinges and to her amazement the door popped right off, Owen caught it and the sound of snarling filled the air.

Owen launched the door into the darkness.

The snarling grew louder and Augusta jumped up and shook her head.

The tendrils of darkness were laughing and wrapping around each other to form a very large imposing man. He had to be at least twice the height of Augusta, wearing foul black armour but Augusta was focusing a lot more on the two massive curved blades in his hands.

"You cannot escape," the man said, his voice rough like he wasn't used to speaking.

Owen stepped forward. "By the power of throne, step aside,"

Augusta was surprised at the sheer tone of authority in his voice even she felt the urge to step to one side even though she outranked him totally.

The man laughed and raised his curved blades. "You will die first,"

The man flew at them.

Augusta pushed Owen to one side.

The man slashed at her. Her armour absorbing the hits.

Augusta couldn't fight. She wasn't that good at it. she was a Queen not a soldier.

The man kicked her.

Augusta fell against a wall. Icy coldness shot into her.

The man leapt into the air. Dark tendrils wrapped around Augusta.

She pushed at them. She couldn't be trapped.

The tendrils pinned her to the wall.

The man went over to Owen kicking him in the chest but Augusta was amazed when Owen didn't show any fear or hate or concern. He looked so determined to live but he had probably been beaten so much over the years this was nothing new to him.

Augusta looked up at the golden orbs of light and gestured the orb should attack the man. The orbs shook itself in a very firm no.

Augusta struggled more and more. She had to escape. The man raised his swords.

Augusta's hand burnt hot and the dagger mark connecting her to Cargo glowed golden and the tendrils burnt away.

Her beautiful dragon was okay and alive and she just had to find him.

Augusta charged at the man. Pinning him against the metal bars.

The man melted through the bars and Augusta fell with him. Her armour became one with the bars.

The man raised his sword to strike.

"Stop!" Charleston shouted.

The man looked around and his focus slipped.

Freeing Augusta from the metal bars. Augusta pulled him back through the still-molten bars.

The man hissed in pain. Owen smashed his fists into the man's wrist. Breaking it and he grabbed one of the swords.

Both Owen and Charleston pressed their three swords against the man's neck and then Augusta realised they were waiting for her command.

She was already their Queen it turned out. She only wished it felt better.

"Where's Cargo the Dragon?" Augusta asked. "And where's King Alfred?"

The man only grinned. "You will never find them,"

"Then may your false gods find you in the afterlife," Augusta said clicking her fingers.

All three swords chomped onto the man's flesh. His corpse melted away into a pool of bubbling oil.

As much as Augusta wanted to hug, kiss and see if Charleston was okay. Time was seriously against them as Augusta heard the thunderous screams of cannons, catapults and crossbows being fired in the far distance.

The army was here and the Lordigomans were clearly prepared so now they had to destroy the defences before everyone Augusta cared about died a horrid death.

Time was seriously running out.

CHAPTER 16

Charleston was so glad that beautiful, sexy and perfect Augusta was okay and that Owen was as well. He still felt so bad for allowing his sweet brother to be taken and beaten. He should have protected him better but the only real way to protect Owen was to kill their father.

And that required a dragon.

Charleston knew that there was only one place in the entire palace that could house a dragon securely so he had gotten Owen and wonderful Augusta to climb up onto the flat stone rooftops of one of the palace's outbuildings and right now they were all standing around a small opening.

One that occasionally shot out fire.

The building itself was a horrible one built out of solid granite that was magically enhanced to make sure no dragons ever escaped and inside from the looks of it, it was nothing more than a massive football stadium without the seats like Charleston had seen in Jasper once or twice.

"There's Cargo," Owen said.

Charleston could see that Cargo really was a beautiful dragon but his light blue scales were dusty and dirty and chipped right now but that was mostly because of the massive iron chains wrapped around him.

Cargo sadly couldn't move his wings, feet or mouth.

Augusta knelt on the ground and held out her hand with the dagger mark. Cargo seemed to sense it and that really impressed Charleston.

"I'm here Cargo," Augusta said. "Tell us what we need to do."

It's about time you peeps showed up. Do you have any idea how badly my joints my hurting because of these damn chains?

Charleston laughed as the words echoed inside his head because it was great to see the dragon was still okay.

Ya need to climb down and free me. There are no guards here and there is, a presence. Like a witch or wizard. I would guess these chains are-

Charleston bit his lip. The words didn't stop naturally and it was more like the psychic link Cargo had established had been sliced with a boiling hot knife or something.

The roof collapsed.

Charleston fell down to the ground and the roof regrew perfectly. Charleston leapt up with Owen and

Augusta next to him.

They all went back-to-back and Owen and wonderful Augusta whipped out their swords that they had picked up on the way over here.

Cargo hissed in pain as the chains glowed bright red. Charleston had to admit it was a clever trick of the magic user here. Put the dragon in so much pain that one of them broke rank and made them all easy pickings.

He was just grateful that Augusta didn't fall for it.

A very short woman wearing a light blue dress made from dragon scales appeared in front of Charleston.

"Beautiful dress isn't it?"

Charleston didn't dare respond as the air crackled with magical energy. The foul woman was playing a game with them and Charleston hated games.

Charleston swung his swords.

The woman clicked her fingers and Cargo screamed as the two swords appeared in his sides.

Augusta broke the formation and they all formed a defensive line between the woman and Cargo. As if that was actually going to do anything.

"Cute," the woman said. "I suspected you would come for the dumb creature but I expected more of a fight,"

Charleston looked around for a weapon of some sort but there was nothing in the building that he could use. He didn't have magic. He didn't have anything.

But he did have his wit and the minds of two wonderful people that he seriously cared about.

"I think your dress is disgusting," Charleston said.

The woman actually looked horrified like the words were a physical wound. Maybe they were.

"I mean darling," Owen said, playing up his so-called gayness by twenty-fold. "I have kissed men with better dresses than you,"

The woman looked so offended and Charleston realised his two swords had fallen out of Cargo.

"And come on woman," Augusta said, "my kingdom's piss poor but even the lowest and poorest plebs don't wear dresses that bad. I mean seriously,"

The woman stumbled back and her eyes were filling with water.

All three of them formed a bullying circle around her and just kept shouting insults about her stupid dress.

"Maybe you should burn it," Charleston said. "Maybe you should just rip it up,"

"No. Please stop," the woman said in-between tears.

Augusta rammed her sword into the woman's chest and the woman gasped as her dress was ripped and her dark red rich blood poured out of her chest ruining it once and for all.

The woman's eyes widened and her entire body melted away.

Owen looked at the puddle of blood, melted

bones and muscles and nodded. "I've heard of fashion magic before and I thought it's a myth. It's when a person with very weak magic creates an item of fashion that is meant to make them look more powerful and over time their ego and magic and life becomes so focused on the item. That when it's destroyed or damaged it kills them,"

Charleston shook his head what a waste of a life.

Excuse me!

Charleston jumped as the words slammed into his mind and then the three of them rushed over to Cargo.

Augusta quickly found the point that all the chains were tied to and the three of them used their swords as levers and pinged the in chains off.

Charleston had a massive suspicion that Cargo had helped them but he liked to believe that he was strong. Especially in front of someone as beautiful as Augusta.

Cargo roared and immense torrents of fire shot out the top of the building and within moments the granite roof shattered.

Cargo shielded the three of them with his wings and then Charleston helped Augusta and Owen aboard before he did the same.

As Cargo flapped his wings and they started flying towards the frontline Charleston had to admit his entire body was tensing because they were one step closer to getting into killing distance of his father.

And that excited him a lot more than he ever

wanted to admit.

CHAPTER 17

Augusta seriously loved flying with Cargo, Charleston and Owen with the wonderfully refreshing air blowing all around them. The sounds of smashing rocks, screams and the smashing of swords echoed all over the City and the sky.

Augusta watched as the rebel/Octogian forces formed a ring of steel around the City making it impossible for forces to break through. They were effectively sitting ducks for the catapults, arrows and more foulness that Alfred's forces were unleashing on them.

"If me and Cargo burn the defences on top of the stone walls. I need you two to attack the ground forces," Augusta said.

Augusta pointed to the hundreds of men and women in golden armour that stood just outside the city walls to make sure her forces didn't even get close to the walls.

"Do it," Owen said.

Augusta felt Charleston hug her tight but not in weakness but because he cared about her and she cared a lot about him.

"Do it please Cargo," Augusta said.

The dragon roared as loud as it possibly could and to Augusta's amazement all her forces cheered in utter fury and they charged.

By the gods did they charge.

Augusta had never seen humans run so fast in all her life. They would be on top of the enemy position within moments. Maybe less than a minute.

Cargo flew over the battlements. Unleashing a torrent of fire.

Burning soldiers alive. Burning catapults. Smashing crossbows.

A loud scream filled the air and Augusta realised it was the same sound as earlier. The enemy were activating the spire defences.

The same defences that had made them all get captured earlier.

Cargo flew to one side as a massive arrow screamed towards them. Augusta loved how he could read her thoughts.

Augusta gripped on harder and Cargo flew low enough over her forces for Charleston and Owen to jump off.

An arrow flew past her head.

Cargo shot upwards.

More screaming of metal gears filled the air and Cargo corkscrewed through the air. Augusta felt like she was about to be sick.

More arrows zoomed through the air.

Cargo roared as he unleashed torrents of blue flame. Within moments one of the spires were melted.

Molten metal pouring down the spire and onto the soldiers outside.

Cargo did the same to the others.

Something smashed into Augusta.

Throwing her off Cargo. Cargo screamed. Racing after her as she fell.

Augusta watched as an immense shadowy black corrupted dragon smashed into Cargo.

The enemy dragon wasn't slowing down. It was chomping. Slashing. Smashing itself against Cargo.

Augusta flew past molten spires.

Augusta screamed louder and louder as she realised she was going to slam into the ground.

Her dagger mark burnt bright white and Augusta felt like she had wings for a moment and she flapped them.

She didn't know how. She only did.

Augusta slowed down and she landed on the hard cobblestone ground with a thud and her wings were gone.

She looked up to see where Cargo was but clearly the wing trick had damaged him. Dragon blood was raining off him now.

Yet Augusta couldn't get the feeling of someone using the enemy dragon as a puppet off her mind. She had no doubt that Cargo had implanted the idea into her head but she was just happy for it.

Augusta looked around, up and down the long white marble street and noticed a woman with long raven hair moving her arms and fingers around chaotically and she was focused on the dragon.

That's when Augusta realised that the black dragon was the one that Cargo had killed earlier. The woman could have taken possession of the body for this defence now.

Augusta charged at her. She had to distract the woman.

Augusta shouted at her. The woman smiled and didn't dare look at Augusta.

Augusta leapt into the air.

Knocking the woman to the ground.

Augusta climbed on top of her. Punching the woman in the eyes.

This magic had to rely on her eye contact. Something that Augusta couldn't allow.

Augusta covered the woman's eyes with her own hands. She didn't want to injure the woman. She might have been a good person.

A magical force gripped Augusta.

It threw Augusta against a white marble wall. Pinning her there.

The woman focused back on the black corrupted dragon. At least it was missing a leg.

Augusta struggled against the magic and she could see how much effort the woman had to use.

That sheer level of effort couldn't be sustained.

Augusta struggled more and more. Trying to kick her legs, move her arms and shake her head.

She saw sweat pour off the woman's face despite how cool it was. The woman shot Augusta a warning look.

Augusta kicked even more and the woman charged over to Augusta.

But it was all that Cargo needed.

He roared in utter fury as the black dragon stopped moving and Cargo slaughtered him.

Bright red dragon blood rained down on the entire city as Cargo slaughtered the enemy.

The woman spun around. Her concentration slipped. Augusta was free.

So she snapped the woman's neck.

Augusta had never wanted to do that and she absolutely hated the sound of the snapping bone but it was needed. It was the woman's life or hers.

Or at least that was what she was going to keep telling herself.

The deafening cheer of thousands of loyal forces echoed all over Lord City as the iron gates were smashed down (probably with some magical help) and now her forces were in the city Augusta just grinned.

It was finally time she killed King Alfred and take the country for herself. If Owen and sexy Charleston allowed her to.

CHAPTER 18

Charleston was actually really surprised that their way to the palace along the white marble road was lined with people cheering, shouting praise and clapping at them as they came to the palace. It was clear that the people loved Augusta and him and everyone else who was a liberator against his father.

And he was even more surprised when the palace guards personally opened the gates for them to come and the five most loyal guards to Alfred had led them to the throne room.

As the large iron doors of the throne room opened, Charleston was expecting to be attacked or something but he was more than surprised to see his weak, pathetic father crying his eyes out. His face twisted in rageful confusion at the sight of his most loyal guards with the rebels, but Charleston didn't care.

His father deserved to die as his tears stained the polished beautifully white sterile marble floor. The key would be making sure his father's blood didn't stain the marble.

Augusta came in and dismissed the guards and then Charleston, her and Owen went over to Alfred.

Charleston wanted nothing more than to kill his father straight away but apparently Augusta wanted to ask a single question first.

Augusta got eye-level with him and she grinned. "Why?"

Alfred went to spat at her but his shoulders rolled forward and for the first time in his life Charleston realised that his father was actually defeated and out of moves.

"I did it out of love for my people. I will not live forever and I need them to have a strong king. Charleston is weak, soft and he will never be a good King. Owen has all the qualities of a king but he's a pussyboy,"

Owen laughed and Charleston realised he really didn't need to keep worrying about his beautiful precious brother, but he wasn't weak. He was a strong person that had fought with the strength of an entire army earlier on the battlefield whilst Augusta had been fighting the corrupted dragon.

"And I wanted your kingdom because of what Jasper is doing. The Emperor is moving his forces against the borders more and more each day. He is growing stronger and stronger and he has his eye fixed on each Kingdom. I needed your mines,"

"And so you started to seed doubt and

corruption in the Freedom Front Barons,"

"You cannot win against them. Octogi is weak. Lordigo will be weakened by your ruler,"

Charleston was surprised when Augusta grinned and whipped out a knife and she cut out his father's tongue.

"The kingdoms will be weak with that attitude. At least that way I don't have to hear your negativity," Augusta said turning to Charleston and Owen.

Charleston knew what she was going to ask next and he actually didn't know if he wanted to kill his own father. Of course his father needed to die but he wasn't sure if he should give the honour to Owen.

Charleston loved it how Augusta grinned at him like she already knew exactly what he was thinking and she passed the wet knife to Owen, and he took it like Augusta really was his Queen giving him a sacred charge.

Charleston laughed as he watched his father's eyes widen in utter terror as Owen rammed the knife into the bottom of his stomach and tore it upwards so all his father's stomach, guts and lungs were exposed.

His father tried to scream but the lack of tongue made that impossible.

"Guards!" Augusta shouted.

Moments later five guards came in and they actually looked horrified. This might not have actually been the best idea Charleston realised because the last thing he wanted was for rumours of Owen's brutality (or worse Augusta's) to spread throughout the

Kingdom and the people start to rebel out of fear.

"Take the body and parade it through the street. Then burn it please," Augusta said.

As the guards did exactly what the Queen commanded, Charleston and Augusta just hugged Owen and he weakly smiled. Charleston had no idea if Owen's act of killing would ever come close to healing the wounds and hours of beatings that his father had given him, but Charleston wanted Owen to know he would always love, protect and treasure him.

Because no one else in life had ever given Owen that before. Until now.

CHAPTER 19

A few hours later Charleston was sitting in his father's old library that stretched on for miles upon miles with white marble bookcases of ancient knowledge, scrolls and leather-bound books that stretched from floor to ceiling. It was such a wonderful library and him and Owen had spent many nights studying here trying to learn everything they possibly could about the world.

The dark brown wooden table Charleston sat at, with Owen next to him wearing a very nice white robe that actually made his brother look at peace, was perfectly cool, smooth and very inviting.

There were candles attached to the walls and other tables that provided more than enough light in the growing darkness as night veiled the sky, and he was very curious as to why Augusta wanted to talk to them both.

There was only one more large brown oak chair at the table so clearly it would be just the three of them, and that was exactly how Charleston wanted it. He didn't want other ears, people or creatures listening to such a thing but he was fairly sure that Cargo would be reading Augusta's thoughts throughout tonight.

And every day going forward.

He actually didn't mind that because Cargo was a great dragon and Charleston honestly believed he might class the dragon as a friend one day, and with reports of Jasper's army on the border, he had a feeling that they were going to need a dragon more than ever.

The silence of the library was eerie as was the smell of musty old books, sweet orange incense and the aroma of chocolate that one of the palace scholars must have been eating when the city was under attack. At least the scholars were hard workers and the palace could be on fire and he doubted they would move out the way.

That was exactly how dedicated those amazing crazy people were.

A few moments later Augusta walked in and sat at the chair wearing a very sexy light blue robe and Charleston forced himself not to stare too much. But she looked absolutely stunning, sexy and Charleston was so glad Augusta couldn't see his lower regions.

"My coronation will be tomorrow," Augusta said, "and as part of it our kingdoms will officially join and become one, if you both consent to it. Then I will have to appoint a Lord Governor of Lordigo to rule it in my name,"

Charleston nodded, now he understood why the meeting had been called.

"It has to be Charles," Owen said. "The law is clear, a gay cannot be King,"

Augusta just looked at him for a moment and Charleston was expecting Owen to jump up and hug her.

"You said *Lord Governor*. Thank you so much," Owen said.

Charleston was so glad that Owen was basically going to be king and at least he managed to keep his promise to Lady Margret. The wonderful woman that had sacrificed herself for him and Gracey, who was busy setting up the new constitution of both kingdoms. Charleston was so glad he didn't have to do that.

"And you Charleston Alfred," Augusta said grinning, "how would you like to become Royal Advisor to me? You would be my bodyguard, have to advise me on matters and you would travel with me to Longmano and Jasper when my power is established here,"

Charleston bit his lip. It was only now that he realised just how much ambition this beautiful woman had, and he also knew exactly how deadly of a game she was getting involved in.

Charleston had had a lot of dealings with Jasper over the years unlike Octogi. He knew exactly how brutal, cunning and murderous that country was.

But Charleston nodded and grinned like a little schoolboy not only because this was the future and he really wanted Augusta to conquer all the human lands to unite them against the orks, trolls and other creatures that wanted to kill humanity. But also because he really wanted to spend more time with this stunning, sexy woman.

Augusta stood as did Charleston and Owen.

"This is going to be the start of a powerful and very fruitful friendship," Augusta said turning to Charleston, "and maybe, partnership,"

Charleston grinned when he heard that because he would honestly love nothing more and whilst there were a hell of a lot of problems ahead of them.

That was next week's problem and tonight and tomorrow was all about celebrating their freedom, their Queen and their brand-new future.

And Charleston was really looking forward to it.

CHAPTER 20

As much as Augusta really, really wanted stunning Charleston to join her back in Octogi and she just wanted to see his amazing body, she sadly had to admit there was a lot of work to do and whilst the past week had been all about cementing her power, her loving grip on the country wasn't perfect yet.

It seriously helped her image when she had personally spent half a day helping the amazing, wonderful people of Grace City and Owen and very sexy Charleston finish the defences around their farms so it was impossible to attack them.

It seemed the entire country loved her for getting her hands dirty. She was more than willing to keep doing that.

But as Augusta sat on the awfully cold dirty golden throne of her kingdom, she smiled as she looked at all the dirty stone that made up her throne room. She had to admit that this was her home, her domain and exactly where she felt safest and the world was a very scary place outside and it was only when she was reading the battle reports that Alfred had been enjoying before his death that she realised exactly what she was getting into.

Augusta was impressed that the cleaners had managed to make the cold stone ceiling seem a little brighter, and in fact everything in the kingdom seemed to be bright.

The experts had finished the sanitation network for the entire country a day ago and all the human waste was washed out far beyond any city or town limits, and then the farmers waited for the waste to rot and then it was used as fertiliser on the fields.

Augusta was really looking forward to next year's harvest because finally all of her people might be fed for a change, and that was only because she was now a ruler of not one but two kingdoms.

And there were still two more to go. The two most powerful.

Augusta had already been visited by diplomats from Jasper and Longmano and even though they had tried to be kind, helpful and supportive. Augusta had loved, absolutely loved watching the fear behind their eyes as they realised that she was coming for them in the end.

Augusta was more than pleased when all the idiot so-called Freedom Front Barons had personally written to her and informed her that they were no more, and they would always only be loyal to her.

She wasn't sure if it was because she gave them a working sanitation system or it was because the barons realised that she would one day control all four kingdoms so there was nowhere for them to go but she didn't care. The result was the same.

Yet Alfred had been right to be scared about Jasper. She had seen reports that counted hundreds of thousands of soldiers, creatures and something called *Steam Powered Tanks* on the border. They wouldn't be able to defend against that so hopefully Gracey would have better luck as she was now travelling to Jasper to calm down the diplomatic tension.

The very last thing she needed was a full-blown war with Jasper whilst her two new kingdoms were barely out of infancy.

A knock on the door made Augusta smile as Savannah in a beautiful blue dress walked in and magicked up a chair for herself. Augusta couldn't believe how great it was to see her again.

"Well you've been busy," Savannah said.

Augusta nodded. "We still have a lot of things to do and thankfully I made it Lordigo law to allow witches and wizards to practice freely unless they harm others,"

Savannah hugged Augusta. "Thank you. I finally get to travel again,"

"It's the least you deserve after all. You managed the kingdom perfectly and gave me time to bring back hundreds of thousands of coins so we finally have money and the kingdom is rich again,"

Savannah grinned at that and Augusta understood why. She could actually start to pay her best friend with real coin instead of shelter, food and water.

"And I managed to bond with a dragon like you always spoke about,"

"Cool. That makes you the first-ever Dragon Rider," Savannah said. "When humanity was first created thousands of years ago, there were dragons working with humans all the time, the dragons mentioned how humans could bond with them but no one managed to,"

Augusta nodded. It was great to know that she was the first of something and hopefully she would also be the very first Queen and ruler of the four kingdoms.

"But I am curious why Alfred didn't use his magic at all on me. I know he was a secret magic user and what was that red crystal that knocked out Cargo?"

Savannah nodded. "The crystal is a very unique form of magically infused Jasper from the highest mountains of Jasper itself, and it's very dangerous. I wouldn't recommend touching it,"

"I ordered for it to be locked away in the dungeon of Lord City."

"Very wise," Savannah said. "And I researched Alfred and when he was younger he was a massive collector of magical crystals. Literal crystalised magic, I think he ate one of them before he saw you so he could appear to be a secret magic user. But he was old, weak and pathetic, that single crystal probably burnt away his insides and he was living on borrowed time,"

Augusta nodded, she was determined never to let that happen again. That sounded horrific.

Savannah bowed as she was about to leave when she looked behind her and weakly grinned at Augusta.

"Your highness, the orks. We might need more additional soldiers from Lordigo. The Orks have broken into the country and they will reach the first city of Octogi in three days,"

As Savannah marched off, Augusta grinned. She would have to send the order immediately because whilst she had bought back five hundred men and women to help defend the human lands against orks, the enemy was clearly stronger than she believed.

But it would be okay. Three days was plenty of time to defeat an enemy so tonight she would simply send the order and the orks would be firmly tomorrow's problem.

Because she was Queen, she was powerful and most importantly she was death to all of her enemies and that was exactly the excellent way she wanted to be thought of.

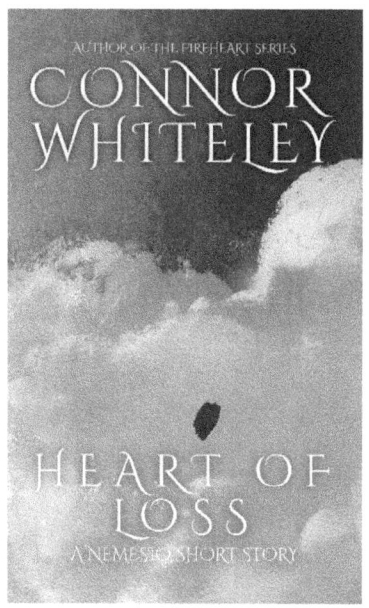

GET YOUR FREE AND EXCLUSIVE SHORT STORY NOW! LEARN ABOUT NEMESIO'S PAST!

https://www.subscribepage.com/fireheart

Keep up to date with exclusive deals on Connor Whiteley's Books, as well as the latest news about new releases and so much more!

Sign up for the Grab a Book and Chill Monthly newsletter, and you'll get one **FREE** ebook just for signing up: Agents of The Emperor Collection.

Sign Up Now!

https://dl.bookfunnel.com/f4p5xkprbk

About the author:

Connor Whiteley is the author of over 60 books in the sci-fi fantasy, nonfiction psychology and books for writer's genre and he is a Human Branding Speaker and Consultant.

He is a passionate warhammer 40,000 reader, psychology student and author.

Who narrates his own audiobooks and he hosts The Psychology World Podcast.

All whilst studying Psychology at the University of Kent, England.

Also, he was a former Explorer Scout where he gave a speech to the Maltese President in August 2018 and he attended Prince Charles' 70th Birthday Party at Buckingham Palace in May 2018.

Plus, he is a self-confessed coffee lover!

Other books by Connor Whiteley:

Bettie English Private Eye Series

A Very Private Woman

The Russian Case

A Very Urgent Matter

A Case Most Personal

Trains, Scots and Private Eyes

The Federation Protects

Lord of War Origin Trilogy:

Not Scared Of The Dark

Madness

Burn Them All

The Fireheart Fantasy Series

Heart of Fire

Heart of Lies

Heart of Prophecy

Heart of Bones

Heart of Fate

City of Assassins (Urban Fantasy)

City of Death

City of Marytrs

City of Pleasure

City of Power

<u>Agents of The Emperor</u>
Return of The Ancient Ones
Vigilance
Angels of Fire
Kingmaker
The Eight
The Lost Generation
Hunt
Emperor's Council
Speaker of Treachery
Birth Of The Empire
Terraforma

<u>The Rising Augusta Fantasy Adventure Series</u>
Rise To Power
Rising Walls
Rising Force
Rising Realm

<u>Lord Of War Trilogy (Agents of The Emperor)</u>
Not Scared Of The Dark
Madness
Burn It All Down

Gay Romance Novellas
Breaking, Nursing, Repairing A Broken Heart
Jacob And Daniel
Fallen For A Lie
Spying And Weddings

The Garro Series- Fantasy/Sci-fi
GARRO: GALAXY'S END
GARRO: RISE OF THE ORDER
GARRO: END TIMES
GARRO: SHORT STORIES
GARRO: COLLECTION
GARRO: HERESY
GARRO: FAITHLESS
GARRO: DESTROYER OF WORLDS
GARRO: COLLECTIONS BOOK 4-6
GARRO: MISTRESS OF BLOOD
GARRO: BEACON OF HOPE
GARRO: END OF DAYS

Winter Series- Fantasy Trilogy Books
WINTER'S COMING
WINTER'S HUNT
WINTER'S REVENGE
WINTER'S DISSENSION

Miscellaneous:
RETURN
FREEDOM
SALVATION
Reflection of Mount Flame
The Masked One
The Great Deer
English Independence

OTHER SHORT STORIES BY CONNOR WHITELEY

<u>Mystery Short Story Collections</u>
Criminally Good Stories Volume 1: 20 Detective Mystery Short Stories
Criminally Good Stories Volume 2: 20 Private Investigator Short Stories
Criminally Good Stories Volume 3: 20 Crime Fiction Short Stories
Criminally Good Stories Volume 4: 20 Science Fiction and Fantasy Mystery Short Stories
Criminally Good Stories Volume 5: 20 Romantic Suspense Short Stories

<u>Mystery Short Stories:</u>
Protecting The Woman She Hated
Finding A Royal Friend

Our Woman In Paris
Corrupt Driving
A Prime Assassination
Jubilee Thief
Jubilee, Terror, Celebrations
Negative Jubilation
Ghostly Jubilation
Killing For Womenkind
A Snowy Death
Miracle Of Death
A Spy In Rome
The 12:30 To St Pancreas
A Country In Trouble
A Smokey Way To Go
A Spicy Way To GO
A Marketing Way To Go
A Missing Way To Go
A Showering Way To Go
Poison In The Candy Cane
Christmas Innocence
You Better Watch Out
Christmas Theft
Trouble In Christmas
Smell of The Lake
Problem In A Car
Theft, Past and Team
Embezzler In The Room

A Strange Way To Go
A Horrible Way To Go
Ann Awful Way To Go
An Old Way To Go
A Fishy Way To Go
A Pointy Way To Go
A High Way To Go
A Fiery Way To Go
A Glassy Way To Go
A Chocolatey Way To Go
Kendra Detective Mystery Collection Volume 1
Kendra Detective Mystery Collection Volume 2
Stealing A Chance At Freedom
Glassblowing and Death
Theft of Independence
Cookie Thief
Marble Thief
Book Thief
Art Thief
Mated At The Morgue
The Big Five Whoopee Moments
Stealing An Election
Mystery Short Story Collection Volume 1
Mystery Short Story Collection Volume 2
Criminal Performance

Candy Detectives
Key To Birth In The Past

Science Fiction Short Stories:
Temptation
Superhuman Autospy
Blood In The Redwater
All Is Dust
Vigil
Emperor Forgive Us
Their Brave New World
Gummy Bear Detective
The Candy Detective
What Candies Fear
The Blurred Image
Shattered Legions
The First Rememberer
Life of A Rememberer
System of Wonder
Lifesaver
Remarkable Way She Died
The Interrogation of Annabella Stormic
Blade of The Emperor
Arbiter's Truth
Computation of Battle
Old One's Wrath
Puppets and Masters

Ship of Plague
Interrogation
Edge of Failure
One Way Choice
Acceptable Losses
Balance of Power
Good Idea At The Time
Escape Plan
Escape In The Hesitation
Inspiration In Need
Singing Warriors
Knowledge is Power
Killer of Polluters
Climate of Death
The Family Mailing Affair
Defining Criminality
The Martian Affair
A Cheating Affair
The Little Café Affair
Mountain of Death
Prisoner's Fight
Claws of Death
Bitter Air
Honey Hunt
Blade On A Train
<u>Fantasy Short Stories:</u>
City of Snow

City of Light
City of Vengeance
Dragons, Goats and Kingdom
Smog The Pathetic Dragon
Don't Go In The Shed
The Tomato Saver
The Remarkable Way She Died
The Bloodied Rose
Asmodia's Wrath
Heart of A Killer
Emissary of Blood
Dragon Coins
Dragon Tea
Dragon Rider
Sacrifice of the Soul
Heart of The Flesheater
Heart of The Regent
Heart of The Standing
Feline of The Lost
Heart of The Story
City of Fire
Awaiting Death

All books in 'An Introductory Series':
Careers In Psychology
Psychology of Suicide
Dementia Psychology
Forensic Psychology of Terrorism And Hostage-Taking
Forensic Psychology of False Allegations
Year In Psychology
BIOLOGICAL PSYCHOLOGY 3RD EDITION
COGNITIVE PSYCHOLOGY THIRD EDITION
SOCIAL PSYCHOLOGY- 3RD EDITION
ABNORMAL PSYCHOLOGY 3RD EDITION
PSYCHOLOGY OF RELATIONSHIPS- 3RD EDITION
DEVELOPMENTAL PSYCHOLOGY 3RD EDITION
HEALTH PSYCHOLOGY
RESEARCH IN PSYCHOLOGY
A GUIDE TO MENTAL HEALTH AND TREATMENT AROUND THE WORLD- A GLOBAL LOOK AT DEPRESSION
FORENSIC PSYCHOLOGY
THE FORENSIC PSYCHOLOGY OF THEFT, BURGLARY AND OTHER

CRIMES AGAINST PROPERTY
CRIMINAL PROFILING: A FORENSIC PSYCHOLOGY GUIDE TO FBI PROFILING AND GEOGRAPHICAL AND STATISTICAL PROFILING.
CLINICAL PSYCHOLOGY FORMULATION IN PSYCHOTHERAPY
PERSONALITY PSYCHOLOGY AND INDIVIDUAL DIFFERENCES
CLINICAL PSYCHOLOGY REFLECTIONS VOLUME 1
CLINICAL PSYCHOLOGY REFLECTIONS VOLUME 2
Clinical Psychology Reflections Volume 3
CULT PSYCHOLOGY
Police Psychology

A Psychology Student's Guide To University
How Does University Work?
A Student's Guide To University And Learning
University Mental Health and Mindset

www.ingramcontent.com/pod-product-compliance
Lightning Source LLC
LaVergne TN
LVHW012113070526
838202LV00056B/5719